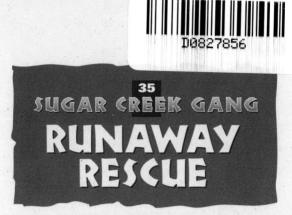

35

SUGAR CREEK GANG
RUNAWAY
RESCUE

Paul Hutchens

MOODY PUBLISHERS
CHICAGO

All Scripture quotations are taken from the *New American
Standard Bible,* © 1960, 1962, 1963, 1968, 1971, 1972,
1973, 1975, 1977, and 1994 by The Lockman Foundation,
La Habra, Calif. Used by permission.

Original Title: *Runaway Rescue at Sugar Creek*

ISBN-10: 0-8024-7038-6
ISBN-13: 978-0-8024-7038-6
Printed by Bethany Press in Bloomington, MN – August 2010

We hope you enjoy this book from Moody Publishers.
Our goal is to provide high-quality, thought-provoking
books and products that connect truth to your real needs
and challenges. For more information on other books
and products written and produced from a biblical per-
spective, go to www.moodypublishers.com or write to:

Moody Publishers
820 N. LaSalle Boulevard
Chicago, IL 60610

3 5 7 9 10 8 6 4

Printed in the United States of America

PREFACE

Hi—from a member of the Sugar Creek Gang!

It's just that I don't know which one I am. When I was good, I was Little Jim. When I did bad things—well, sometimes I was Bill Collins or even mischievous Poetry.

You see, I am the daughter of Paul Hutchens, and I spent many an hour listening to him read his manuscript as far as he had written it that particular day. I went along to the north woods of Minnesota, to Colorado, and to the various other places he would go to find something different for the Gang to do.

Now the years have passed—more than fifty, actually. My father is in heaven, but the Gang goes on. All thirty-six books are still in print and now are being updated for today's readers with input from my five children, who also span the decades from the '50s to the '70s.

The real Sugar Creek is in Indiana, and my father and his six brothers were the original Gang. But the idea of the books and their ministry were and are the Lord's. It is He who keeps the Gang going.

PAULINE HUTCHENS WILSON

1

It was a very lazy, sunshiny early summer afternoon, and I was sitting on the board seat of the big swing under the walnut tree, thinking more or less about nothing. I never dreamed that, before the week would pass, I'd be head over heels in the middle of the red shoe mystery.

My reddish brown mustached father had just climbed down our new extension ladder, which had the Collins name painted on it. He'd been checking the top of the swing to see how safe it was, and he said, "Well, Son, you don't need to worry. Everything up there is all right. Just don't let the whole Sugar Creek Gang swing on it at one time."

He took the ladder down, slid the two sections of it together, and carried it toward our truck, which at the time was standing in the shade of the plum tree near the iron pitcher pump. There he lifted that ladder as if it was made of feathers instead of aluminum and laid it in the back of the truck. He was very proud either of our new ladder or of his powerful biceps. I couldn't tell which.

He climbed into the truck's cab then, started the motor, and began to drive toward the gate that leads out onto the gravel road.

"Where you going with that ladder?" I

called to him. He was just driving past the mail-box that had "Theodore Collins" painted on it when he called back to me, "One of our neighbors wants to borrow it for a few days."

With that, he was off down the road, a cloud of white dust following him.

I stood up on the board seat of the swing and pumped myself one- or two-dozen times and then sat down to coast, enjoying the feel of the wind in my face and the flapping of my shirt sleeves. Swinging like that gives a boy one of the finest feelings he can have—even if he hardly ever gets to have it very long if his folks are at home.

In fact, that very second Mom called from the east window of our house for me to come and help her with a little woman's work. She wanted the house to have a good cleaning before she left for Memory City tomorrow to spend a week at my cousin Wally's house.

It was while I was dusting the lower shelf of our lamp table that I noticed the birthday book in which Mom keeps a record of all the names and birthday dates of people she sends cards to every year. Just out of curiosity, I leafed through to see whose birthday would be coming soon and gasped in surprise when I saw Mom's own name. Then I remembered her birthday was next Saturday, the day she would be coming home from Memory City.

That meant I'd better set my brain to working and think of something nice to get for her—something extra special.

Mom must have heard me gasp, because she looked up from the kitchen floor where she was spreading wax on the linoleum and said through the open door, "Anything wrong?"

I started whisking my dustcloth a little faster and whistling and hardly bothered to answer, saying with a half yawn, "Oh, nothing. Just something I thought of." And I watched for a chance to put the book back where it had been.

Anyway, it was while I was on my way Saturday afternoon to get a birthday present for Mom that Poetry and I stumbled onto the mystery—the red shoe mystery, that is.

The very special entirely different kind of gift I had decided on was up in the hills not far from Old Man Paddler's cabin. We were trudging happily along when what to my wondering eyes should appear but somebody's red leather slip-on shoe lying in the mud at the edge of the muskrat pond.

That spring-fed pond, as you may already know, is about halfway through the swamp. The sycamore tree and the mouth of the cave are at one end, and the woods near Old Man Paddler's clapboard-roofed log cabin are at the other end.

Even from as far away from the shoe as I was at the time, which was about thirty feet, I could tell it wasn't anybody's old worn-out, thrown-away shoe. It looked almost new, as if it had been worn hardly at all. It had a low heel and was the kind and size a teenage girl might wear.

I was so surprised at what I was seeing that I stopped and stood stock-still, and Poetry, who was walking behind my red wagon in the path, bumped into it with his shins.

For a few seconds, Poetry staggered around trying to regain his lost balance. Then he lost it completely, upsetting the wagon at the same time, and scrambled, rolled, and slid down the slope toward the pond's muddy bank. And also toward the red shoe.

"What on earth!" his ducklike voice managed to squawk at me. "Why don't you let me know when you're going to slam on your brakes like—"

"Look!" I exclaimed. "Right behind you at the edge of the pond! There's a red shoe. There's been a murder or a kidnapping around here somewhere!"

As soon as I said that, I began to think that probably that was what actually had happened. Somebody had kidnapped a girl and was taking her along the path through the swamp— maybe to the haunted house far up in the hills above Old Man Paddler's cabin. When they stopped here to rest a few minutes, the girl had broken away from him and started to run. She had stumbled over something, maybe her own feet, had fallen, and, like Poetry, had rolled down the slope. Her shoe had gotten stuck in the mud and slipped off when she tried to pull it out. But she had kept on running.

I suppose one reason my imagination was running away like that was because the swamp was a very eerie place, even in the daytime. That spongy, tree-shaded, sometimes-flooded tract was where the six members of the Sugar Creek Gang had had quite a few exciting and dangerous adventures in the past.

I never will forget the dark night Big Jim's flashlight spotted old hook-nosed John Till's head lying out in the quicksand about thirty feet from the high path we were always careful to stay on when we were going through. That is, we *thought* it was his head lying there but found out a split second later that the rest of him was fastened to it. Somehow he had gotten off the only path there is and had been sucked all the way up to his chin in the mire.

That was a feverish time, I tell you. His calls for help and his scared eyes in the light of the flashlight were enough to make any boy's hair stand on end.

And it was in this very swamp that Dragonfly, the pop-eyed member of our gang, had first seen a fierce mother bear wallowing in the mud on a hot summer day the way hogs do in a barnyard wallowing place.

One of our most nerve-tingling experiences happened right here at this muskrat pond when my cousin Wally's copper-colored mongrel, Alexander the Coppersmith, had a fierce under-the-surface battle with a snapping turtle —the biggest turtle there ever was in the Sugar Creek territory.

So, with these adventures in the history section of my mind, it was easy for me to imagine a screaming girl's frantic struggle with a fierce-faced kidnapper, maybe on the grassy mound I myself was on right that second.

With my mind's eye I could see her wrestle herself out of his clutches, stumble, and roll down the bank, where her shoe came off in the mud. She didn't dare stop to get it and put it back on but kept running on through the swamp to the woods and on to Old Man Paddler's cabin or in the other direction to the sycamore tree and the cave.

That was as far as I got to think along that kind of scary line, because Poetry, who had picked up the shoe and had a different feeling about it than I did, started to quote one of the hundred and one poems he knew by heart:

"For want of a nail, the shoe was lost;
For want of a shoe, the horse was lost;
For want of a horse, the rider was lost."

I'd memorized that poem myself when I was in the fourth grade.

There were quite a few things in our school readers that were supposed to teach us things that were good for a boy to know. This one taught us how important little things could be. If the horse's owner had noticed when the horseshoe had lost a nail and had a new nail put in, the horse wouldn't have lost the shoe and wouldn't have gone lame and stumbled and fallen, and the rider wouldn't have gotten killed. A boy ought to be careful about little things such as having his mother sew up the small torn places in his shirt and not dropping lighted matches anywhere.

That lost-and-found shoe wasn't very large, but it could be a very important clue. "Be careful!" I called down the knoll to Poetry. "Don't wipe off or smudge up any fingerprints!"

"Who cares about fingerprints?" he called back. "Come on down and take a look at these *footprints!*"

I left my upset wagon where it was and clambered backwards to where Poetry was. "What footprints? Where?" I asked him, not seeing anybody's tracks.

"Right there!" he said. "At the edge of the water!"

I looked again and saw what he was stooped over and pointing at with his right forefinger. "That," I objected, "is a muskrat's track!"

I was looking at a three-inch-long, web-footed track—several of them, in fact—at the water's edge, and I knew that the webbed tracks had been made by the hind feet of one of the cutest wild animals there is in the Sugar Creek territory, a chuckle-headed, beady-eyed, stocky-bodied, nearly naked-tailed rodent.

Next, my eyes searched all along the bank of the pond where we'd found the red shoe. I saw only muskrat tracks—not one single human being's tracks anywhere.

"I guess we have stumbled onto a mystery," Poetry was willing to admit. Then he yawned, as if it wasn't too important, and, handing the red leather shoe to me, he added, "Let's get going. We have to get the tree dug and balled and back and set out before your folks get home."

Now my mind was divided. An hour ago, when we'd started from home, pulling my red wagon along, it seemed I was on the way to do one of the most important things a boy could do —plan a big birthday surprise for his mother.

In fact, Dad and I had planned it together and had managed to keep it a secret for a whole week. It had been easy to keep the secret that long because Mom had been away from home that long. And when she would get back to the Collins place late this afternoon, the surprise would be waiting for her in the backyard just outside the dining room window.

The cute little two-foot-high blue spruce tree Poetry and I were on our way up to Old Man Paddler's to get would be standing green and straight and proud halfway between the two cherry trees at the end of the row of hollyhocks that grew along our orchard fence. Would my wonderful mother ever be pleased!

That's why Poetry and I were taking the path through the swamp instead of the shortcut through the cave. The cave actually comes out in the old man's cellar, but we never could have pulled the wagon through the cave.

As I said, my mind was divided. I had a birthday surprise to hurry up and get for Mom, and maybe I had a kidnap mystery to solve. Somebody somewhere—maybe close by—needed a boy's help.

"How," I demanded of Poetry, as if he knew and didn't want to tell me, "how in the world did the shoe get *here?* There isn't a human being's tracks anywhere except ours!"

"It fell here, of course. How else?"

"From where?" I asked and looked up at the overhanging branches of a big elm. "Shoes don't grow on trees!"

"All right," he said loftily. "I'll get going on the mystery myself. Somebody's got to solve it, and it may just as well be the best detective in the whole county."

He meant himself, Leslie Thompson, which, even though I knew he was joking, was almost the truth. His mind was always ferreting out the answer to some knotty problem.

"First things first, though," Detective Thompson began, and the tone of his ducklike voice told me he had taken charge of the mystery and I was to take orders from him from now on. "You carry the shoe. I'll pull the wagon this time, and you follow behind. Keep your eyes peeled for anything suspicious such as a red dress with a girl in it and another red shoe with a girl's foot in it."

Of course, Poetry was right about our needing to get going. We had to get going to get done what we had to do, shoe or no shoe, girl or no girl.

Even though in a few minutes we were quite a way from where we had found the red shoe and were hurrying along on the winding narrow path, leaving the pond behind, my mind was still back where it had been. Who, maybe last night, maybe early this morning, maybe only a few hours ago, had been in such a hurry that she had lost a shoe and hadn't dared stop to get it?

Also, Poetry's little ditty was repeating itself in my mind:

> *For want of a nail, the shoe was lost;*
> *For want of a shoe, the horse was lost;*
> *For want of a horse, the rider was lost.*

I wasn't thinking of a lost horseshoe, though, but of a lost, left red shoe and the girl who had been wearing it.

I kept my eyes peeled in a circle of directions as we hurried along, looking and hoping to see a red dress with a girl in it. Whoever she was, did she need the kind of help two boys with work-and-play-hardened muscles could give?

Where was the other shoe, and why had this one been tossed away, if it had? I decided to wipe off the mud, using the gunnysack we'd brought along in the wagon for balling the tree.

The shoe, as I'd first decided, was almost new. "Hey!" I gasped to Poetry. "Look at the sole! It doesn't have any mud on it! Only on the side! She *wasn't* wearing it when it got left in the mud! It wasn't even on her foot!"

But Detective Thompson wasn't impressed. "Like I said," he called back over his shoulder, "it fell or was thrown from somewhere!"

Ahead of us I could see more light through the trees. That meant that soon we'd be through the swamp, into Old Man Paddler's woods, and on the way to his cabin and the stream behind his woodshed where the spruce tree would be waiting for us. In a little while, I started to think, we'd—

And that was as far as I got to think. At right that second, as plain as a white cloud in a clear blue sky, I heard a bloodcurdling scream, the kind a wildcat makes when it's hunting or maybe like a mountain lion makes. It was that loud.

"Wildcat!" I whispered to Poetry, who'd stopped stock-still so suddenly that I whammed into the wagon with my own shins, and we almost had another upset.

"Not a wildcat!" he corrected me. "They do their roaming and hunting in the morning and evening twilight. In the hot afternoons they sleep. Besides, last summer we killed the only wildcat there ever was in this part of the country. Remember?"

I remembered, all right, one of the most dangerous adventures we'd had in our whole lives. But right then I thought of something I'd not thought of for a long time. "She had two little kitten wildcats, didn't she? And we took them to the zoo in Memory City?"

"That's what I said," Poetry countered. "First, we killed the mother, and then we gave her babies away."

"Yeah," I came back, "but whoever heard of

a family of wildcats without there being a father as well as a mother! Old Stubtail's babies had to have a father!"

Already I was cringing at the idea, and my eyes were alert for a reddish brown fur coat with a wildcat in it. "There! There it is again!" I half whispered, half yelled to Poetry. This time the sound wasn't a scream, though. It was a wolflike cry that was half howl and half laugh with a little mournful wail all through it.

"It's a loon!" Poetry decided emphatically.

"But it can't be. We've never seen any loons around here. Only when we've been on camping trips in the northern lake country!"

But sounds such as the two bloodcurdling howls we'd just heard had to come from something or somebody. I wished Big Jim were with us with his rifle. Or Circus with his bow and arrow. Or even Little Jim, with his long walking stick, which he'd made himself and always carried. Or Dragonfly, who was good with his slingshot. Anybody, just so there would be more of us if we accidentally did run into a situation that would need the whole gang to solve it or to fight it out.

I was actually trembling inside as, with the red shoe in my hand, I hurried along after Poetry. I just knew there was something wrong somewhere. Somebody somewhere needed our help.

2

When we finally reached the old man's cabin, we found the door closed and locked. There was a shipping tag hanging by a string on the knob, the kind of tag people tie on sold furniture in a store or to something that's being sent by mail or express or freight.

We knocked first, as we always do when we visit anybody. That is one of the Sugar Creek Gang's courtesy rules: never open anybody's house door and walk in without knocking. That also was one of our family rules. Even when we are inside the house, we knock first on a closed door to find out if the person in the other room would rather have privacy. The only person in our family who goes into any room anytime she wants to, if we let her, is my three-year-old sister Charlotte Ann.

As I was saying, we knocked first on Old Man Paddler's front door. Then, when nobody answered the knock, Poetry tried several more times, while we listened for any sounds from the inside.

When there was still no answer and our ears didn't hear anything, Poetry complained, "I thought you said he told you he'd be here to show you which tree to dig. I got my shins

17

cracked on your wagon and rolled down the hill for nothing!"

By that time I was studying the shipping tag. "Here!" I cried excitedly. "There's a note." It was a note in the old man's trembling scrawl.

I'm sorry not to be at home, boys, but early this morning I decided to take that trip to California I've been telling you about. The tree, as I told you last week, is behind the woodshed. I've tied a red ribbon on the one you're to dig.

You'll find the spade in the woodshed. I left the door open and unlocked. The latch is set so all you have to do is just shut it when you put the spade away, and it'll lock itself.

The note was signed with the old man's initials, "S.P." which I knew meant Seneth Paddler, although the same letters could have meant Sarah Paddler if she had been alive.

She was buried in the very old grass-grown cemetery at the top of Bumblebee Hill. Their two boys were buried there, too, and someday the old man himself would be. In fact, his tombstone was already there and had his name on it and the date he was born. His death date won't get chiseled on until he dies, which all the boys of the Sugar Creek Gang hope won't be for a long time. In fact, we hope the kind, long-whiskered old man won't ever die.

He'll have to, though. Everybody does, our minister says. Not wanting to won't make any difference, so everybody had better be ready.

Standing there now, reading the carefully scrawled note, I remembered something the old man had said to us the day he promised me the tree for Mom's birthday surprise. The whole gang was in his kitchen at the time. We had just finished a drink apiece of sassafras tea, which he makes for us every time we go up to see him.

On the oilcloth-covered kitchen table was part of the manuscript of a book he had been writing, which I could see he'd named "The Christian After Death." Beside the manuscript was an open Bible and quite a few other books, some open and some not. Several of them were like some books we had in our library at home, books called commentaries. My parents use them all week every week, studying their Sunday school lessons. Both Mom and Dad are teachers.

Little Jim swished down the last of his tea. Standing with his cup in his hand and his eyes focused on the book manuscript, he piped up in a mouselike voice and asked, "What do people do after . . . after . . ." He stopped and nodded toward the manuscript.

Everything was quiet in the house for what seemed several minutes. Then the old man lifted his head, and his snow-white hair, which had just had a shampoo and was silky and shining, was prettier than I'd ever seen it. He looked out the window in the direction of the wood-shed and beyond. Then he answered Little Jim.

"True believers in Christ keep right on liv-ing. Death for them, boys, is like being trans-planted. Take that little spruce tree Bill's giving his mother for her birthday. It's not going to die. It's just being moved. You dig it up here and set it out there. And it keeps on living."

That was one of the prettiest things I'd ever heard anybody say. It flashed through my mind in a hurry while I was still standing reading the note on the shipping tag.

"What's wrong?" Poetry interrupted my thoughts to ask. "You've got tears in your eyes!"

"Have I?" I answered and was surprised to notice that my eyes were stinging a little, the way they do when I get smoke in them.

In a few seconds we were on our way to the woodshed. There we found the door open, as the note said, and the spade leaning against the old man's workbench. I noticed he had been building something or other, but he had all his tools put away in the places made for them on the wall above the bench. My mind's eye took a quick picture of everything I saw, and seconds later I was outside.

The cute little two-foot-tall blue spruce was only a few feet from the noisy brook that flows behind the woodshed. It was a good thing the old man had tied the red ribbon on it, because there were about seven other small trees close by, and we could easily have picked the wrong one.

Right away we were digging, using the shovel we'd brought and the spade from the woodshed. I knew exactly how to transplant a small tree, since I'd read how in a book I'd borrowed from the Sugar Creek Library. A library is what my dad calls "a thinking boy's best friend."

"Not too close to the tree," I cautioned Poetry, "or you'll cut off some of the obliques." I felt proud of myself because I knew what obliques were.

He grunted a kind of lofty answer, saying, "I know. I read the book myself. First growing out from the taproot are the primary roots, then the secondaries, then the tertiaries. And from these there are thousands of obliques, and from the obliques, millions of capillaries as fine as hair and even finer root hairs by the billion and—"

"Stop! Don't tell me everything I already know!"

"One thing you don't know, though," he countered.

"What's that?"

"It's only through the billions of root hairs that the tree can drink. And I'm thirsty." With that, he tossed down his shovel and then was on his hands and knees beside the brook, drinking like a cow. While he was there, he spotted the red shoe I'd dropped nearby and said, "I wonder if it'll hold water and how much?"

But I quickly stopped him from using it for a drinking cup.

Poetry, his thirst satisfied, grunted himself to his feet and started quoting one of his many poems, one I happened to know myself.

"I chatter, chatter as I flow
  To join the brimming river;
  For men may come and men may go
  But I go on forever."

"Tennyson," I said. "Tennyson wrote it."
And he grunted back, "Yeah, Tennyson."
The fast flowing brook beside us certainly didn't act as if it had a worry in the world. It tumbled cheerfully along on its way toward Sugar Creek, whose spring floods had been over for more than a month.

"I wish *I* could run around all day and not even have to get out of bed to do it," Poetry remarked. Then he added, "But I guess a brook or a creek or a river is about the only thing in the world that can do that."

That was an old joke I'd heard years ago when I was little.

Pretty soon we had a deep trench dug all the way around the tree at the end of its obliques. We were about ready to start balling the roots when I heard the old man's cabin door open and saw four boys come tumbling out, chattering, laughing, playing leapfrog, and whooping it up.

It was the rest of the gang: Big Jim, our fuzzy-mustached leader; Little Jim, the littlest one of us; Circus, our acrobat and the best boy archer in the county; and last of all, spindle-legged Dragonfly, whose nose is allergic to more smells than anything. He also has the noisiest sneeze of any of us.

I stopped, straightened up with a shovelful of dirt in my shovel, and called, "How'd you get in the house with the door locked?"

"We came through the cave." Dragonfly sneezed, then added, "Big Jim has the keys. Old Man Paddler gave 'em to him on his way to town."

Big Jim held up a key ring to prove what Dragonfly had said was the truth and explained, "He stopped at our house, and my folks drove him to the bus station."

It certainly felt fine to have the rest of the gang with us. We needed a few extra muscles anyway to help ball the tree and especially to help lift it into the wagon, since the ball of dirt was going to be very heavy.

"We get to come up every other day to water the flowers and shrubs," Dragonfly said. He drew back with his sling and let go a small stone in the direction of the old man's spring, where there was a tin can standing on a rock shelf. His rock just barely missed the can.

"Let me show you how to do it," Circus said.

Carefully, Circus took aim with the bow and arrow he'd brought with him. The homemade arrow flew straight as a bullet, whammed into the tin cup, and sent it tumbling into the spring reservoir.

That's when I noticed the arrow had a long

string fastened to it, and the string had unrolled from what looked like a plastic drinking cup fastened to the bow. In a second, Circus was winding the string back onto the drinking cup, and the arrow followed along toward us on the other end.

Guessing I was curious about the plastic cup attached to the bow, Circus explained, "It's a homemade reel for bow-fishing. This is spawning season for carp and suckers, and I'm going to shoot a few for our hogs. You guys see any in the muskrat pond?"

We hadn't, but we had seen something else—a girl's red leather slip-on shoe. I was about to tell Circus and the rest of the gang but didn't even get started, because Circus was so proud of his homemade bow-fishing outfit that he cut in on me.

Holding up his outfit for us to study, he explained, "First, you take a plastic cup like this, stick a heated knife blade clear through it near the bottom, and then you use the slits to strap the cup onto the bow. Like this, see?"

It was hard to "see" when I wanted to talk myself.

"All you have to do," he said proudly, "is run the end of a kite string through the screw eye here at the nock and along the length of the arrow to the arrowhead. You fasten it, and you're ready for business. When you've stalked a carp or a school of 'em, you just take aim, shoot, and *wham!* you've got a fish!"

When he finished, I still had only a foggy

idea of how he'd made his outfit. I did see that he'd driven a slender nail through one of his arrows just above the point, driving it at a sharp angle so that, where the nail's pointed end came through, it made a barb for fastening the string.

Each one of the four had brought something with him: Circus, his bow-fishing outfit; Little Jim, his walking stick; Big Jim, Old Man Paddler's ring of keys; and Dragonfly, his slingshot.

Dragonfly had also brought something else. What it was I discovered a little later when I saw him starting to play with a red shoe, tossing it up and catching it as it came down!

"Hey!" I exclaimed to that little rascal. "That's a clue to a kidnapping or something! I found it back in the swamp at the edge of the pond!"

"You did not!" he said saucily and kept on tossing up the shoe and catching it as it came down. "I found it myself at the mouth of the cave!"

I looked in my wagon, where I'd put the red leather slip-on shoe Poetry and I had found, and what to my wondering eyes should appear but the shoe itself, still there. Dragonfly had a *right* shoe instead of a left.

"Where'd you say you found it?" I asked him.

That's when he spied the shoe in the wagon and made a dive for it. "I wondered where the mate was!" he cried happily. "Now I've got a whole pair!" He plopped himself down beside Tennyson's brook, took off his sneakers, and in a flash was up and strutting around in the red shoes.

"Those are *girl's* shoes!" Poetry scoffed. "You want to look like a girl?"

Dragonfly stopped, glanced in the direction of the afternoon sun, got a messed-up expression on his face, and sneezed a long sneeze that could have been heard almost as far away as the swamp.

For a second I'd forgotten what Poetry and I came up there to do. My mind was all tangled up in the mystery again. Now we had *two* lost-and-found shoes!

Dragonfly's noisy sneeze must have given Circus an idea. Right away he flapped his arms at his sides the way our old red rooster flaps his wings before he crows. Then he cupped his hands to his lips to make a megaphone out of them, threw back his head, and let out toward the sky a bloodcurdling scream like a wildcat's or a mountain lion's. It also sounded like a half-scared-to-death woman in danger of her life. It was the same sound Poetry and I had heard when we were in the swamp.

Before I could gather my scattered thoughts, Circus cut loose with another high-pitched cry, this time like the mournful wail of a northern lakes loon.

It certainly was deflating. It was like having a blowout and losing all the air in a tire on the car you are riding in to have the hysterical cries

26

I'd been afraid of back near the muskrat pond turn out to be just one of the gang mimicking a wildcat and a loon. Circus had probably made the sounds just before they went into the cave to go to Old Man Paddler's cabin the back way.

Well, it took some of the danger out of our mystery, but it didn't solve it. We still had a pair of girl's red shoes on our hands. Or feet.

And Dragonfly was still strutting around in them near Tennyson's brook. I noticed he was walking with a limp.

"What's the matter?" Little Jim asked him. "One shoe got a nail in it?"

The question started Poetry in again.

"For want of a nail, the shoe was lost,
  For want of a shoe—"

That was as far as he quoted before Dragonfly fired back at Little Jim, "One of them's too short. Feels like there's something stuffed in the toe."

With that, he plopped himself down on the grass again, whisked off the left shoe, and took out of its toe a folded piece of paper, which he gave an over-the-shoulder toss toward the brook. It landed in a riffle and was whisked away downstream, dancing over the covered rocks and around the uncovered ones as if in a hurry to get as far away from us as possible.

"You goof!" Poetry cried at Dragonfly and started racing after the wad of paper. "That might have been a clue!"

Even before Poetry finished saying that, I was scooting downstream after it myself. But Circus, faster than either Poetry or me, swished past us and in a flash caught up with the clue or whatever it was. He reached out and scooped it up.

3

I don't know what I'd expected to find in or on the wad of paper Dragonfly had tossed into the brook. It could have been something very important, or it could have been nothing at all.

But the way we scampered to Circus and gathered around in a semicircle to see what he had found was like something I see happen every day in our barnyard. A mother hen finds a nice juicy fishing worm near the pitcher pump, clucks to her family of little chickens to come to dinner, and a half-dozen or more fluffy, cheeping, hungry baby chicks come running from every direction and gather around her, bills first.

I hadn't any sooner started pecking away with my eyes on what Circus had just unfolded and smoothed out than I decided it wasn't worth all the hurrying we'd done to get it.

"It's nothing," he said, bursting my hope balloon all to smithereens.

In front of our twelve eyes, all focused on the smoothed-out clue, was nothing but about a fourth of a newspaper page. I guess maybe I'd been hoping that on the wadded-up paper would be a note the girl had written and stuffed into the shoe before she threw it away. If anybody found it, they could read the note, which would maybe say, "Help! I'm being kidnapped!" Or maybe it would say something else exciting, such as telling who she was and where she'd come from and who her kidnapper was.

We had a quick conference there beside the half-balled spruce tree to see if anybody had any ideas as to who or what or when or how or why whatever was going on was going on, if it was.

Little Jim's mouselike voice managed to get heard above the rest of ours. "It's like the fairy story of Hansel and Gretel, whose parents didn't want them anymore and took them out into the woods to lose them. Hansel filled his pockets with little white stones and dropped them all along the way to leave a trail for him and his sister to get home by. I'll bet she dropped her shoes like that to mark the kidnapper's trail and—"

Little Jim stopped as if he knew his idea wasn't any good, even before Dragonfly broke in to scoff, "Who in the world could follow a trail made by only two dropped shoes? Besides, who said her parents didn't want her? Maybe she didn't want her parents!"

Poetry's idea wasn't much better. He proposed, "That wad of paper shows one thing anyway. The shoes didn't belong to her!"

"Didn't belong to her!" I challenged him. "How in the world do you know that?"

"Because," he quacked back, "they were too large for her. She had to stuff wads of paper in them so they'd fit tight enough to stay on." He quickly stooped, lifted Dragonfly's left foot, and whisked off the red shoe.

Dragonfly lost his balance and fell sprawling on the grass, almost rolling into the brook.

"See?" Poetry began in a tone of voice he tried to make sound like a lawman's. "This shoe was worn by a little girl about eight years old. She was the youngest child in the family, and her older brothers and sisters made her feel just how little she was all the time. They were always calling her the baby in the family. Little Marian felt so humiliated and angry that she decided to run away from home. One morning early, she slipped into her older sister's room, put on her red shoes, went out the side door, and scooted silently across the road and into the woods and—"

"Hold it!" Big Jim charged in with his voice to stop Poetry. "Everybody calm down and talk a little sense!"

Little Jim, whose Hansel and Gretel idea hadn't been any good, broke in with another. "One foot was smaller than the other. That's why she stuffed paper in only one shoe. She was crippled in one leg, so one foot was a lot littler than the other and—"

Well, we certainly weren't getting anywhere with our ideas. We'd better finish balling our tree. I had to hurry to get its primaries, secondaries, tertiaries, obliques, and its millions of root hairs in the ball of dirt, carefully and tightly wrapped in the gunnysack we'd brought.

Then we'd ramble along through the swamp and all the way home and get it set by the orchard fence at the end of the hollyhock row between the two cherry trees before Mom and Dad and Charlotte Ann got back from Memory City.

We still didn't know what Big Jim thought about the shoes. Maybe he'd been waiting to get our different ideas, then put them all together and make out of them a brand-new idea better than any of them. It seemed our ideas were only a lot of wet wood being thrown onto a smoldering campfire.

But when Big Jim came out with his idea, it was like throwing on the fire only a little bigger wet log than ours had been. Here is what he just that second said:

"One thing we do know, gang, is that whoever she was or is, she reads the *Indianapolis News*. See here?"

We all looked where he was pointing, and I saw the name of the paper and that it was dated just three days ago.

"Did she live in Indianapolis then?" Little Jim asked.

"Who knows?" Big Jim answered.

Things certainly looked strange. We had on our hands a pair of red shoes, one of them found at the edge of the pond in the swamp and the other at the mouth of the cave. How in the world had they gotten there? Who had stuffed a wadded-up piece of the *Indianapolis News* in one of them, and why?

Because we couldn't do anything by doing nothing, we decided to get going on the tree and to think while we worked. My thinking father had taught me that was good for a boy. "It makes the work easier, and you get it done before you know it," he had told me maybe fifty times.

Circus, whose father had maybe taught him to sing while he worked, was humming along while we were finishing. It was one of the prettiest songs there ever was. Some of the words were, "I think that I shall never see a poem lovely as a tree."

We knew we could never get the wagon with the tree in it down Old Man Paddler's cellar steps and into the cave. And even if we could, we couldn't pull it through the long, narrow winding passageway to the cave's mouth. Those of us who were going to push and pull the wagon would have to go back the long way. The rest could take the shortcut through the cave and be waiting for us when we arrived. From the cave and the sycamore tree we could all go on to my house.

But Big Jim decided for us, saying, "We'll stay together." He had a grim expression on his fuzzy-mustached face, and I noticed the muscles of his jaw were tense as if his teeth were pressed together and also as if his mind was set.

Secretly, so that Little Jim wouldn't hear me, I asked Big Jim, "You scared about something?" and he whispered back, "You just don't find one girl's shoe lying in the swamp and another at the mouth of the cave unless there's something to think about anyway. And *sh!*"

I knew what the *"sh!"* meant. It meant "don't use the word *scared* around Little Jim."

Well, we would have to go back into the cabin again to lock the cellar door that led into the cave. We decided that, while we were inside, we would look around a little to see if the old man had closed all the windows to keep out the rain and had drawn the drapes and blinds to keep the hot sun from pouring in and fading any of his rugs. Maybe he'd overlooked something. There would have to be some light for his plants, too.

I glanced toward the afternoon sky to see how much time we had yet before sundown and was surprised to see some mountain-high, cream-colored cumulus clouds, the kind Dad calls thunderheads. It might even rain before we could get home, I thought.

As soon as we had all stopped for a drink apiece at the old man's spring, we started to the cabin. We had gotten as far as the steps leading to the door when we were startled by a sound we hardly ever heard around Sugar Creek. It was like a tornado tearing along through the woods.

"Airplane!" Circus exclaimed.

But that was before we saw it.

"It's a whirlybird!" Little Jim cried gleefully. His cute little face looked as if somebody had turned on a light behind it.

We saw the helicopter for only a few seconds. Then it disappeared, its horizontal propellers carrying it low above the trees and hills, swinging northwest up the deep gulch and out of sight.

"There's your answer," Poetry whispered to me. "That's where the shoes came from. I told you they fell from somewhere. Somebody up there didn't want them and just threw them out. One shoe landed by the sycamore tree at the mouth of the cave and the other in the swamp at the edge of the pond."

"What on earth!" I said and got corrected by Dragonfly.

"Not what on earth! But what in the sky!"

I could tell by the expression on his face that he thought what he'd said was funny. And he could tell I *didn't* think it was by the expression on mine.

The whirlybird hadn't any sooner disappeared over the horizon in the direction of the gathering clouds, than it sounded as if it was coming back again.

It not only sounded like it, but it looked like it. The helicopter swung back into view over the rim of the highest hill, circling and zigzagging and all the time getting nearer the open area where Old Man Paddler's cabin was—and, of course, where *we* were.

Poetry, still acting like a detective, took on a teacherlike tone of voice as he said, "That, gentlemen, is a flying machine held up by a stream of air driven downward by propellers turning on a vertical axis. By vertical, of course, we mean perpendicular. By perpendicular we mean pointing to the zenith—straight up, to you who may not know what the zenith is. You take that helicopter coming yonder—"

"No," Big Jim cut in on him to say, "*you* take it. In fact it looks like we're all going to take it in another minute or two."

Sure enough, that flying machine with its propellers whirling on a vertical axis was circling lower now and in a few minutes would be down far enough to land.

The helicopter landed in the open space near the old man's spring, and two strange men stepped out. One of them was red-haired and short, and the other wore a pilot's cap. They both lowered their heads as they hurried toward us under the whirling blades of the helicopter. The man with the cap held onto it to keep the wind from blowing it off.

I thought there was what looked like a lot of worry on the red-haired man's red face. He called out to us above the whirring of the slowing helicopter motor. "You boys seen anything of my daughter around here anywhere? A girl about fourteen years old? In a red dress?"

Detective Leslie Thompson's answer was guarded, as if he didn't trust the men at all. "Maybe we have, and maybe we haven't. What's she wanted for? What's she done?"

After all, how did we know she was his daughter? Maybe the men were kidnappers.

The other man cut in then, and his voice was sharp, "She's wanted for rabies treatment.

Her pet squirrel bit her on the hand yesterday, and we've just found out it was rabid. If we don't find her and get her to a doctor, she'll die!"

You should have seen the frightened look on the red-haired man's red face when the pilot said that.

Also, you could feel Detective Thompson change his attitude.

Of course, we had not seen a girl, but we knew one had been around here somewhere last night or early this morning because of the shoes we had found. It took us only a few seconds, with all our voices helping a little, to tell the men what we knew and for Dragonfly to quickly take off the shoes he had put on again and thrust them toward the red-haired man.

Dragonfly said, "This is how come we know she was here. We found them—one of them down there in the swamp by the muskrat pond and the other at the mouth of the cave!"

It was really pitiful the way that red-haired father clasped those shoes to his breast as if they were his daughter and he had just found her. He let out a sob, saying, "Oh, Elsie! My Elsie! What have I done to you!"

There wasn't any time to lose now. I could feel myself already on a chase, looking for a girl in a red dress, trying to find her and get her to a doctor for the Pasteur treatment, which is what they do for anybody bitten by an animal with rabies. I knew because I want to be a doctor someday and had read about it in a book I borrowed from the thinking boy's best friend.

"She's got to be around here somewhere," I managed to say between about a thousand other words flying back and forth. "Or else why did she lose her shoes here?"

And that's when we found out that she *didn't* lose her shoes here. Her father himself had lost them. He had dropped them accidentally out of the helicopter early that morning when they'd been flying around searching the area for some sign of her.

Elsie had left the shoes at the covered bridge in Parke County, where—with three other young people—she'd been in a terrible car accident. Two of the four had been killed and a third was in the hospital right that minute for serious head injuries. At the scene of the wreck, they'd found Elsie's red shoes, the pair she had probably been wearing when she climbed out the window of her home and went on a wild ride with her friends.

The girl's worried father, who had been telling us the sad story, wound up by saying, "I just know she's somewhere, wandering around in a daze, maybe with amnesia or terribly hurt."

"How come she left just her shoes at the bridge?" Poetry asked. "Wasn't there any other clue, such as a handkerchief or anything? Or maybe a handbag?"

All our thoughts were interrupted then by a voice coming in on the helicopter radio. It was the police, saying a girl of Elsie's description had been seen in one of the sandstone ravines of Turkey Run State Park.

And that's why we were soon alone again with only a wagon and a balled spruce tree, while the whirlybird was climbing fast toward the high horizon in the northwest, skimming the tops of the trees and hills on the way toward the sandstone gorges of Turkey Run State Park.

All we had left of what we'd thought was going to be a real mystery for us to solve was the small wad of paper we'd found in one of the shoes.

We still didn't know why it had been in there, but Little Jim's guess was as good as any. He said, "I bet both her shoes were a little too loose, and she had a wad of paper in each one. The other wad fell out when she had the accident or maybe when the shoes fell out of the whirlybird."

There was a dark brown cloud in my mind somewhere, a great big ache that made me wish and wish and wish they'd find the girl and get her to a doctor before it would be too late.

In my mind I could see what might be happening to her if the squirrel that had bitten her had really been rabid. First, the place where the bite was would start to hurt, and then her voice would get husky, and she wouldn't be able to swallow easily. Then she wouldn't be able even to stand the sight of water because of the terrible pain in her throat. After that she would become paralyzed, and, if she didn't get a doctor's help quickly, she would die, as the helicopter pilot had said.

Knowing all that about what rabies does to people, it seemed I ought to do about the only thing I had left to do. As I stooped at the spring to get another drink, I heard myself whispering, "Please, heavenly Father, help them find her! Help the doctor, if they get her to him. And if she's not a Christian, help her get a chance to get saved, especially if she's not going to get well, so she can go to heaven."

Poetry must have guessed what I hardly knew myself I was doing. A few seconds later, when we were all on our way to the cabin again to lock up before going home with the balled tree, he slipped his hand through my arm and whispered to me part of a Bible verse I'd learned once, "'Is anything too difficult for the Lord?'"

I knew there wasn't, but I also knew that most of the hard things God did for people, He used other people to help Him do it—people like a doctor or a nurse or even a boy.

In a little while we were inside the cabin, and that's when our mystery came to life in a new way and landed us all right in the middle of it. While I was upstairs in the loft, checking on things up there, I stumbled onto a real clue. In fact, I stumbled *over* it. When I reached for the banister to brace myself from falling, my hand missed it and I went down.

Whatever it was I'd stumbled over went scooting across the floor to the head of the stairs and *bumpety-bump, ploppety-plop-plop* all the way to the bottom.

What on earth! I thought as my wondering eyes looked down the steps and saw what it was. A red plaid suitcase was lying on its side, where it had finally stopped under the old man's kitchen table. Even in the fleeting glimpse I'd just had, I noticed it had a red handle and its locks were brass like those on the suitcase my mother had taken with her to Memory City.

While I was shuffling my way to my feet, I exclaimed down to the rest of the gang, "He left in such a hurry, he forgot part of his luggage! You suppose we ought to rush it to town and ship it to him?"

In seconds I was downstairs.

Big Jim had already picked up the red plaid suitcase and set it on the table. All of us started giving different suggestions about what to do with it.

"I'll bet he left all his spending money in it," was Dragonfly's idea. "We'd better open it and find out, and if he did, we can—we can—"

"We can what?" I asked.

Dragonfly lifted his hands, palms up, and shrugged as he so often does when he doesn't know anything or doesn't want to say.

Little Jim piped up then. "Maybe it's got his book manuscript in it—the one about Christians keeping right on living after they're dead. They're not dead at all but are in another place like a spruce tree. Maybe he wanted to write more on it out there."

Suddenly Poetry quacked out his detective-like idea, a different thought than any of us had had up to then. "Look, gang, who said it was Old Man Paddler's suitcase? Maybe it's not his at all. Do you notice what color it is? That's the same color as somebody's red shoes! Maybe it belongs to whoever the shoes belong to!"

He had no sooner startled us with that than I heard from somewhere in the house a half-smothered sneeze. I looked at the faces of the rest of the gang, and there wasn't a single left-over sign of any of them having sneezed or trying to smother one. My mind told me the sound had come from upstairs where I had just been.

My ears told me something else also. One of the windows up there was being opened— maybe the one I knew led out onto the roof of the old man's back porch!

And then there was a noise on the roof itself, a clatter like the one on the lawn in the poem "The Night Before Christmas," where it says, "Out on the lawn there arose such a clatter, I sprang from my bed to see what was the matter."

When several of us sprang to our feet to dash out and around the corner of the cabin to see what was the matter, I glimpsed what Poetry had warned me back in the swamp to be on the lookout for—a red dress with a girl in it! Except that she was wearing bright red pants instead. She was poised at the farther edge of the porch when I first spotted her. Her hair was the color of one of the mountain flowers called Indian paintbrush. We'd seen thousands of them on our trip to the Rockies one summer.

Quicker than a firefly's fleeting flash, the girl was over the edge of the porch and gone. When I glimpsed her again, she was gliding like a bird toward the woodshed, the clump of baby spruce, and Tennyson's brook. A fraction of a second later—she was moving fast—she disappeared into the thicket of shrubs growing there.

What on earth! In fact, double what on earth!

4

We didn't wait until Elsie, if that was who she was, reached the brook and leaped over and disappeared into the thicket. Half of us were already after her as fast as we could go, and I heard my voice calling, "Stop! Don't run away! We want to get you to a doctor. Your pet squirrel had rabies!"

But our yells and scared screams didn't make any more impression on her than six rocks thrown into a Sugar Creek riffle could stop the water from racing on.

Circus, still carrying his bow and arrow, reached the woodshed first, ran past, and in a flash was leaping over a narrow place in Tennyson's brook. I was third in the chase, right behind Big Jim, with Poetry, Dragonfly, and Little Jim bringing up the rear.

Even as I passed the open woodshed door, I was reminded that we had to clean the old man's spade we'd borrowed and put it back in its place. Out of the corner of my eye, I noticed the rick of fireplace wood, the wheelbarrow, and the old man's workbench, where he sometimes made outdoor furniture to sell to people. Above the workbench on the wall were his carpenter's tools—a handsaw, several different kinds of hammers, a brace and bit set. On the long workbench was a coil of new rope, and a carpenter's square leaned against the back wall beside an aluminum level. I had seen these things earlier when we went in there to get the spade in the first place.

"Stop! Elsie, stop!" I was yelling.

I suppose all our voices yelling after the runaway girl were kind of like Mr. McGregor's voice yelling for Peter Rabbit to stop—it only scared Peter more and made him run faster. There was only one difference. Mr. McGregor was angry at the innocent rabbit for getting into his garden, but we certainly weren't angry at Elsie, if that was who she was.

Even as I ran, catching every now and then a glimpse of red through the bushes, I realized that red was a good color for hunters to wear so that somebody else hunting could see them and not think they were some kind of game and shoot them.

It was hard to believe a girl could run that fast. She was keeping ahead of our fastest runner, Circus, who, still with his bow and arrow, was like a hound on a hot coon trail. He was leaping over fallen logs, dodging brush piles, and ducking under overhanging branches but not catching up with her.

All the time we were getting higher, heading toward the rocky hills and the haunted house far ahead of us. If she kept going the direction she was going now, pretty soon she'd reach the narrow gulch with its sheer drop-off.

"We'll catch her now," Poetry puffed from behind me. "That's a dead end."

"No, it's not!" I panted back to him. "Don't you remember? The old dead ponderosa blew over in a storm last year and made a bridge across the gulch!"

"That's what I said," Poetry puffed. "It's a dead end. If she crosses the fallen tree to the ledge on the other side, she can't go any farther forward or up or down!"

My mind's eye was in the history section of my mind, remembering the excitement of the wildcat chase we had here and the fight my cousin's dog, Alexander the Coppersmith, had on that high ledge with a fierce-fanged colt killer. Both the wildcat and Alexander fell over the edge and down, down, down to the rocks below at the bottom of the gulch, and both of them were killed in the fall.

If a dog and a wildcat could fall that far and both of them be killed, so could a girl!

Right then there was a noise in the sky, and I looked up quickly, expecting to see the helicopter again. I hoped it was, because maybe the girl's father could call down to her to stop running away and let them take her to a doctor for rabies shots. But there wasn't a sign of the whirlybird. Instead, there was a lead-colored sky with some of the clouds looking pretty fierce, as they do when there's going to be a lot of wind and rain.

Another thing I remembered right then was that sometimes, after a heavy cloudburst higher in the hills, a wall of water comes rushing down the ravine, sweeping everything away.

Once I'd seen a jackrabbit down there all of a sudden wake up to the fact that there was going to be a flash flood. He made a dive for the cliff wall, started up, missed his footing, and landed in a tangle at the bottom again. Before the rabbit could get out of the way, the wall of water hit, and he was swept downstream over the rocks. I never did find out whether he drowned.

But maybe I didn't need to worry about a flash flood. Not more than every few years was there a cloudburst big enough to send a wall of water down like that. Besides, nobody was down at the bottom of the gulch now, anyway.

I heard Circus up ahead of us yelling, "Don't do that! Don't go across! That's a dead end! You get over there on that ledge, and that's as far as you can go!"

Big Jim's deeper voice yelled, too.

And even though I couldn't see the girl right then, I could guess where she was. "Your pet squirrel—it had hydrophobia, and we've got to get you to a doctor!" I half screamed.

Then I saw the red plaid blouse again, and the girl in it was already halfway across the narrow tree bridge on her way to the ledge on the other side. In a few seconds she'd have worked her way across to where there were four feet of ledge, several twisted juniper trees, and a sheer cliff wall. In the wall was the deep hollow that had been the wildcat's lair. I didn't like to think about what was below.

For the first time then, I heard the girl's voice. She screamed back to us, "You want to make me go back home, and I won't do it! I'll never do it!"

For a second, she almost lost her balance. She swayed this way and that, her arms swinging. That's when I saw the bandage on her right hand, and I knew why it was there!

In only another little while, she had balanced her way all the way across to the ledge side. Now she would see that she really was at what Poetry called a dead end. She could go only maybe twenty feet to the right and only about ten feet to the left, which was as far as the four-foot-wide ledge went in either direction.

In front of her was the deep depression in the wall that had been old Stubtail the wildcat's lair. There was a very narrow, rocky, almost straight-up-and-down way to the bottom of the gorge, which Stubtail had used, but it wasn't safe for any human being to try, especially since most of it had been washed out in last year's cloudburst. Not a one of the gang had ever dared try it.

Anyway, there Elsie was, caught in a trap. She turned and stood in her red blouse and red pants, looking across at us, her back to the wall. Her eyes were kind of wild. She was like a fox at bay with a pack of hounds closing in on her. It was ridiculous, the thought of a runaway girl being an animal at bay and the six members of the Sugar Creek Gang that many hounds ready to rush in upon her and tear her to pieces. It was ridiculous because all we wanted to do was help her.

We were all at the edge of the gorge now on our side of the ponderosa bridge only about twenty feet from her.

"Please!" Big Jim said. "We're your friends. We don't want to hurt you! We want to help you. Your father was here a little while ago in a helicopter. Maybe you heard it. He says they've found out your pet squirrel that bit you was rabid and you have to get to a doctor or . . . or . . ."

Big Jim hated to say the word I knew he had in his mind, but I knew it was the truth.

"Your hand!" I called. "Has it begun to hurt yet? Real bad, I mean?"

"Come on back across," Big Jim coaxed her. "We'll get you to a doctor as quick as we can!"

But she just stood and stared at us, and I noticed she was shaking with sobs. "It's my fault they got killed!" she cried. "I kept telling them to drive faster. It's my fault! My fault!"

And there on the ledge at the place where the deep depression was in the cliff wall, she sank down and broke all to pieces in her mind and cried and cried.

Well, a boy can be terribly disgusted with a girl about a lot of things and wonder sometimes if girls even belong to the human race, but when one of them cries with a broken heart, he wants to be her friend and do something to really help her. It seemed I wanted to go racing across the log bridge and hand her my handkerchief. I might even want to help wipe the tears away or maybe say something that would take the pain out of her hurt heart. I certainly didn't expect her to listen to Big Jim.

But all of a sudden she gritted her teeth, pressed her left hand on her right one where the bandage was, and grimaced as though she was in pain. I thought I knew what that meant. It was the first thing a person noticed if he'd been bitten by a rabid animal—the bite began to hurt more than at first. Then she looked across at us, started toward the tree bridge, stopped, looked over the edge at the ragged outcroppings of rock below, and quickly drew back.

"She's scared!" Poetry hissed into my ear.

A second later, she herself said, "I'm afraid! I don't think—"

"We'll help you!" Big Jim's kind voice called over to her. "Wait a minute!"

Big Jim and Circus both started across. They were only halfway when I heard a different kind of noise—not a helicopter's whirling wings and throbbing motor, not a rumble of thunder, not a wild wind in the trees, but a *cracking* noise. The rim of the ledge on the other side, which held up the far end of the ponderosa trunk, was starting to crumble. A half-dozen rocks broke loose and slid down into the gorge. The big old tree staggered and trembled.

"Hurry!" Big Jim yelled back to Circus. "The bridge is going down!"

It was too sickening to even hear, let alone look at. I stood and cried on the inside as I imagined two of the best boys there ever were in the world being dashed to pieces on the rocks below. Then I saw Big Jim leap off the end of the tree and onto the ledge, balance himself, and fall on his knees there, safe.

Circus, still several feet from the ledge, made a flying leap, too, as the log bridge went down—but his jump was too short. Ahead of him, his bow and arrow landed on the ledge. Maybe that was why he was late in getting himself across. He'd taken a fleeting second to toss his bow-fishing outfit first.

It was too horrible to think about, but it had to be faced. Our Circus, our acrobat, the boy who had the best singing voice in Sugar Creek, who was always singing church songs about the Savior, might never sing again.

Even at a time like that, though, when the crying inside of you is enough to tear you to pieces, when your voice is stuck in your throat and you can't say a word, you *can* do something. You can do what a visiting minister once said in our church—you can "flash pray." You can send up wordless prayers that go up as fast as lightning comes down. And that's what I realized I was doing.

Almost before the dust of the falling rock cleared away, I was looking over the ledge to see what had happened to Circus, expecting to see our suntanned, curly-haired acrobat down at the bottom, mangled and bleeding.

Instead, I heard him call up to us, "I'm safe! I'm all right!"

Then I saw him, only about fifteen feet below. He was on a very narrow outcropping, half lying down. He was holding onto the twisted trunk of a windblown juniper that was growing out of the side of the ravine wall. His hat was gone, and his hair was blowing in the wind.

The wind! I thought. The wind was already sweeping up the gulch, and in a little while the storm would hit!

My parents had been trying to teach me that you just can't let your mind go to pieces and be ruled by the way you feel. "You're a thinking boy!" Dad had told me many times. "You have a good mind. When you're in an emergency, *think!*"

But how can you think when you can't think? I thought right then.

I was glad that Circus's life was saved, but all three of them over there were in an emergency. There wasn't any way for Elsie and Big Jim to get up the sheer wall of the cliff or down to the bottom. If they *could* get down, there was a way to get back up on our side. We knew that because we'd all gone down to the bottom to get Alexander the Coppersmith's body and bury it. Later, we'd all gone down to dig it up and take it to Tom the Trapper's dog cemetery beside the haunted house.

There had to be some way to get them all down so they could get back up.

There had to be, but it looked as if there was only one way.

"We've got to get a helicopter," Little Jim called out. "Somebody in a helicopter could let down a rope with a noose on it, and you could step in one at a time and be pulled up."

It wasn't a good idea, though. Big Jim said that it wasn't, almost before Little Jim finished saying it. "The whirling propellers would strike against the ravine wall, and they'd never be able to let down a rope long enough to reach from away up yonder to away down here!"

But Little Jim's idea was like a seed planted in good Sugar Creek garden soil. The word *rope* seemed to stick in Elsie's mind. She surprised us by saying, "This old juniper over here is alive and green! If it's well rooted, we could tie a rope to it and get down that way!"

I could hardly believe my ears. I could see she was still scared, and I wondered how she could think that clearly. I also noticed she was still holding onto her right hand with her left, and I remembered why we were all in the middle of this emergency in the first place.

Rabies! I thought. *Her pet squirrel was rabid!*

There was a roll of thunder then, nearer than any of the other thunders had been.

Well, it had taken ideas from all our minds to finally come up with the right thing to do—and do quickly. One thing was in my mind. We had to have a rope, a long rope, long enough to reach from the juniper growing on the ravine ledge all the way down to near the bottom or to an outcropping they could stand on and work their way down from there.

Somewhere in my mind was a picture of a coil of rope, but where had I seen it? Where? And then I remembered. It was on the workbench in Old Man Paddler's woodshed.

Right away I yelled my idea to the gang and just as quick got Big Jim's order to get going.

Run! my mind told me! And my dad's words were like a wind behind me, pushing me, putting wings on my feet as I sped down the long slope toward the old man's cabin and the open door of the woodshed. Over fallen logs, dodging brush piles, ducking overhanging tree branches, swerving around rocks, leaping narrow gullies, I hurried.

Two worried thoughts were driving me: We had to get Elsie to a doctor quick so that she could be given the treatment for rabies. And we had to get the three of them—Big Jim, Circus, and Elsie—to the bottom of the gorge and up and out again before there was a flash flood!

We had to!

There was a real wind at my back, but so far it hadn't started to rain. Rain, even if it wasn't a cloudburst, would make everything harder. The noise in the treetops meant wind, I knew, even though I kept hoping the helicopter with the girl's father was coming back.

If the gang could just get her across the gorge and back down to the open space near the old man's spring, the helicopter could swoop down and whisk her away to the doctor. Otherwise, we would have a long, hurried hike through the cave, leaving my balled tree behind to come back for later, and a race to Poetry's house to get his parents to rush Elsie to town in their car.

Hurry, hurry, hurry!

The cabin was in sight now. I could see both it and the woodshed below me. But the wind was getting wilder, and my hair was getting in my eyes—that's how I realized my hat was gone. Maybe it had been blown off quite a while before.

But in a few seconds I'd be there, in the woodshed and out again with the coil of rope and panting back up the slope to the rescue.

What a wind! Big Jim and Elsie could work their way back inside the old wildcat's lair and not get blown off the ledge, but could Circus hold onto his outcropping and the little juniper beside him?

That's when I heard a loud *bang!* It was almost like a shot. It was also like the sound of our stable door slamming when there was a hard wind.

Now I was there. Like Peter Cottontail, I whisked around the corner of the woodshed to the open door. But the door wasn't open! It was shut!

The door that had the latch already set so that all we would have do, when we finished with the old man's spade, was to shut it and it would be locked—that door was shut now!

As I grabbed the knob and turned it and pulled on it, I realized the truth. The door had locked! And inside on the workbench was the rope we absolutely had to have—and quick!

5

The woodshed door was closed and locked. The rope we absolutely had to have was lying inside on the workbench! Three people were depending on me for help. One of them had to have that help in the fastest hurry anybody could get it for her!

It certainly wasn't any time to let my feelings rule me—at least not the kind of feelings I had right that minute. Now was a time to think.

Part of a Bible verse I'd learned when I was just a little kid had come to my mind as I'd been flying down the hill—"Ask, and it will be given to you; seek, and you will find."

Also in my mind was a story I'd read about a brother and sister being chased by an angry goat. The goat was getting closer and closer every second. "Let's stop and kneel down and pray!" the little sister said, but her thinking brother had panted to her, "Let's not. Let's *run* and pray!" And that's what I'd been doing.

I couldn't ask God to break one of His own laws of nature by unlocking the door for me, but I could ask Him to help me do what the second part of the Bible verse said. He could help me find a way to get the rope.

Even while I was thinking that, I remembered the wide window just above the workbench. If I could get that open, I could climb in and out again.

I ran around the woodshed, looked up at the window, which I knew slid sideways to open, then spied a cement block near the woodshed corner. I grunted with it to just below the window and a second later was standing on it, working frantically. If I could pry the window open even a crack, I could maybe slide it open far enough to squeeze myself through.

Standing on the cement block, I could see the coil of rope. I saw I could reach it even without climbing in, if I could get the window open far enough.

But even before I'd worked a minute, I realized I'd never get it open that way. The old man had painted the trim and the ledge. There had been a lot of rain lately, and it was swollen shut tighter than if it had been glued.

Even before I did what I knew I was going to have to do, I wrestled with my conscience about how much it would cost to put in a new pane of glass. Also in my mind was the thought that Old Man Paddler had entrusted his place to us to look after. It was an honor to be trusted like that when, all over the country, so many boys were acting as if they didn't have good sense, breaking into vacant houses and into homes when people were away, stealing and destroying property, and doing a lot of what the newspapers and police called vandalism.

What you're going to do is not vandalism, my good sense told me. *And you can save enough out of your allowance to pay for a new pane for the window.*

The heavy stick I'd picked up went against the window glass.

Crash!

A few more quick strokes with the club took several jagged pieces of broken glass out of the way of my arm, and I was ready to reach in for the rope.

The wind caught at me so hard then that it took my breath away. Trees were swaying, and the water pail at the old man's spring blew off the table there and went rolling and bouncing across the open space toward the cabin, where it hit against the porch.

Well, it just didn't make sense that I wasn't tall enough even on the cement block to reach in and get the rope, but that was the way it was.

I looked around. I had to have a box or something bigger to stand on, and I saw one over on the nearby hillside all by itself. I left the window, made a dash for the box, and stood stock-still when I saw that it was one of the old man's beehives. He had a half-dozen hives all over the countryside on different people's farms where there were fields of clover and lots of other flowers for making honey.

But there was another cement block behind the hive. I worked it loose out of the ground and rolled it and carried it down to the woodshed. I set it on top of the first one, stepped up, thrust my arm through, felt around for the rope, and grabbed it.

Then I was off like a streak, panting and hoping and quoting the second part of the Bible verse on prayer, the part that said, "Seek, and you will find." I had asked, and God had answered, but He had put the answer where I had to look for it and work for it.

Swish, rush, hurry, run like a deer—over fallen logs again, swerving around brush piles again, dodging low-hanging tree branches, clambering up steep slopes. Last year's fallen leaves made a crunching sound under my feet, and, overhead, dark clouds scowled down at me. Most of the time it was a race against the wind, which I knew would be blowing harder than ever up where the gang was.

Had it already begun to rain away up in the hills far above and beyond the haunted house?

It seemed to take me twice as long to get back as it had to get to the woodshed in the first place. When I finally arrived, gasping and panting, the wind was wilder than ever. Big Jim and Elsie were still on the narrow ledge a few feet from Stubtail's lair. Below them, Circus was still on the outcropping, half lying down and half sitting astride the twisted juniper trunk.

"What on earth took you so long?" Poetry asked. "You had time enough to go clear home!"

I wasn't in any mood to be scolded when I had been—it seemed to me—a pretty smart boy and especially when it seemed that with the very special answer to my very special prayer I had been alone with God somewhere, doing everything just right.

I didn't even bother to answer. I was getting the rope ready to throw it across.

"Stop!" I was astonished to hear Elsie call out to me. "If you miss, it'll be lost, and then what will we do?"

I stopped with my arm behind me, about to throw the coil of rope in my hand. It *was* heavy, I realized, and what if I didn't toss it far enough?

I looked to Big Jim now, backed against the cliff wall, his hands clinging to a crevice, his shirt sleeves flapping in the wind. "How can I get it to you?" I asked.

His answer didn't make good sense at first. "Tie your end of the rope to that little elm sapling behind you!"

"Do what?" I yelled back, astonished. How in the world could my tying one end of the rope to a sapling on my side of the gorge get the whole rope across to the other side?

In a few seconds, though, he had shouted a little good sense into my right-that-minute dull mind. I was to tie my end to the elm, wind the rest of the rope into a coil, and then toss the coil across.

The reason? It was as simple as two and two always make four, even if they are added by a thickheaded boy! If my toss wasn't far enough or hard enough, the whole rope wouldn't land down in the bottom of the ravine on Alexander the Coppersmith's first grave!

Its end secured to the elm behind me, the rope was flying through the air with the greatest of ease toward Big Jim and Elsie, more than twenty feet across from me.

But only *toward*. Not *to*. My throw wasn't hard enough or far enough. The wind, which could toss a kite on high and blow the birds about the sky as it says in one of Poetry's poems, blew against the rope, and it was almost three feet short of reaching the other side. It unwound fast and wound up in a long, straight line below us. It was, I noticed, almost long enough to reach the bottom. If it was that long from our side, it'd be that long from Big Jim's. That was good.

I pulled it back up and tried again. And again. And again. Each time, it wound up unwound thirty feet below us.

I saw Elsie's set face, her left hand holding her right, and the scared look in her eyes, like a rabbit's when it's caught in a boy's snare and is waiting for the boy to decide whether to kill it or loosen the snare and let it go free.

"It's raining!" Little Jim cried, but I could hardly hear him for the clap of thunder that exploded in my ears at the same time. I could feel the rain, though, and I could hear the wind in the trees.

Circus yelled up to Big Jim then, "You can *pull* it across! Get my bow and arrow and shoot the arrow to the other side! It's got fifty feet of kite string on the drinking-cup spool. The string's fastened to the arrowhead and at the nock. Shoot it across to Bill. He can tie the rope to it, and you pull it across!"

And that is what Big Jim did.

The arrow from Circus's homemade bow-fishing outfit whizzed past us, landing about ten feet behind me. As quickly as I could, I tied one end of the rope to it, and in even less time than it takes me to write it for you, Big Jim had pulled the rope across to where he and Elsie were.

Seeing the rope stretched all the way across gave Dragonfly another idea. "Now we've got a rope ladder! It would be quicker to come across hand over hand than to let yourself down hand over hand and have to climb all the way back up again on our side!"

For two minutes that seemed like seventeen, we argued back and forth about what to do now. The more we talked and worried, the more time was passing.

It was Elsie's bandaged hand that decided for us. She *couldn't* swing herself across. Maybe Big Jim could make a noose for her foot and by wrapping the other end of the rope around the juniper could ease her down, but what if she couldn't hold on long enough?

Dragonfly, who was always coming up with ideas we couldn't use, came up with one right then. "If we had a real ladder, and if it was long enough, you could cross on that!"

Poetry heard him and scoffed, "Even if we had one, how could you get it stretched from here to there?"

And that's when that spindle-legged, crooked-nosed, sneezy little guy showed that he did have a bright mind even if he didn't use it most of the time. "They could pull it across. We'd fasten our end of the rope to the top end of the ladder, and all they'd have to do is just pull it across."

"We don't *have* any ladder!" I countered.

That's when Elsie surprised us by saying, "Why don't you use the ladder at the cabin?"

"What ladder at the cabin?" Poetry exclaimed.

And my mind exclaimed the same thing. As many times as we'd visited the old man, we'd never seen any ladder except a very old stepladder, which wasn't more than six feet tall. Elsie had probably seen that when she was there.

"That old stepladder wouldn't even reach halfway!" I said across to her, and I was right.

But I was also wrong, because she called, "There's a long one around in the back! I used it to climb onto the back porch roof!" Even as she said it, I noticed she was swaying a little as though she was dizzy.

Well, I knew the old man's six-foot stepladder certainly wasn't long enough for anybody to use to climb up onto his high back porch roof. "You *sure* there was another ladder there?" I asked her.

"Sure I'm sure."

And that, my mind told me, was the only answer. If there was a ladder there—a long enough one, and if it was light enough to carry—it was our last chance. Something else was in my mind, also, and it was *Seek, and you will find.* Maybe the rope I'd fought my way down to the cabin to get had been only part of the way to save Elsie. The ladder was the other part.

"You'd better hurry!" she cried worriedly.

That's when I noticed that she was holding her right hand with her left again. Then she swayed, staggered toward the edge of the ledge, and sank down. Big Jim went quickly to her and grasped her arm.

"She's f–f–fainted!" Little Jim stammered.

I tried to remember what I knew about the way rabies worked, but I wasn't sure what kind of symptoms came next after the pain where she had the bite. In my memory there was something about the patient not being able to stand loud sounds and his voice getting husky and it being hard to swallow. There was also shortness of breath and foaming at the mouth and paralysis.

One thing I did know was that her voice wasn't husky, and there wasn't any sticky-looking saliva on her lips. At least I couldn't see any.

Big Jim dragged her back from the rim of the ledge where she had fallen and into the hollow in the cliff wall.

And right then the storm really struck. The wind and thunder and lightning, which for quite a while had been getting worse, all of a sudden broke loose as if nature had gone mad. It was as if it had made up its mind that a gang of boys trying to save the life of a runaway girl hadn't any right to even try it. Maybe the girl

who had climbed out her home window at mid-
night and gone on a wild ride and whammed
into a bridge and killed two teenagers and sent
another to the hospital had to be punished for
what she had done.

But I knew that God is in charge of nature
and people and everything. Sometimes He
does let us get into tough spots. But as the verse
says, if His people seek His help, we'll find it.
And right then we needed His help a lot.

One thing was sure, we had to have a ladder and quick. And we had to go and get it.

"What kind of a ladder was it?" I yelled
across to Elsie, wondering if it was an old-
fashioned, heavy wooden extension ladder or
one made of aluminum like ours at home,
which would be easy for four boys or even two
to carry.

But Elsie was still in a faint, and Big Jim was
bending over her. I could hardly see them
through the driving rain.

6

Rain, rain, go away,
  Come again some other day.

That was part of a poem we'd had in the second reader. There was also a poem in it about the wind:

I felt you push, I heard you call,
I could not see yourself at all . . .
O wind a-blowing all day long,
O wind that sings so loud a song.

But the rain couldn't be ordered around like that, and the wind wasn't singing any song. In less than a minute and a half, Poetry, Little Jim, Dragonfly, and I were as wet as drowned rats.

Even as we streaked down the hill to the cabin and the ladder, I carried in my mind's eye a picture of Big Jim back up there on the ledge, pulling Elsie with him back into the depression in the cliff to get out of the downpour. Circus's cheerful voice had called out just as we left, saying, "Don't worry about me! As long as my horse doesn't throw me and I can keep holding on, I'll be all right." Then he yelled above the storm, "Let 'er rain!"

I knew he was brave and had good sense. If he could, he'd stay with one leg on each side of the twisted juniper trunk, even though the top of the tree was tossing in the wind like a bucking bronco at a rodeo.

It didn't seem necessary for Little Jim and Dragonfly to get any wetter and maybe blown over in the wind and hurt on a stump or something, so when we passed an overhanging rock and all stopped a few seconds to get our breath, I told them to stay there. Then Poetry and I hurried on down the same trail I'd been on and back on already.

"It's an *aluminum* ladder!" Poetry cried when we sloshed around to the back of the cabin and saw it. It was not standing against the porch roof edge but was blown over and on its side against the rock wall that surrounded the old man's patio. If it had been blown *over* the low wall, it would have been thirty feet below.

"That's *our* ladder!" I yelled.

Now I knew what Dad had done with the ladder that day last week when he loaded it into the truck and drove away with it. He'd driven the extralong way around through Harm Groenwald's lane to Old Man Paddler's cabin so the old man could paint his woodshed and the cabin. And here it was, just waiting for us to carry it up to where Big Jim, Elsie, and Circus were waiting to be rescued.

I tell you it was a long, hard climb with that ladder, even though it was only about half as heavy as a wooden ladder would have been.

The rain swooshed down on our bare heads. We could hardly see where we were going and maybe wouldn't have known except that we knew the right direction was uphill instead of down. A half-dozen times we had to stop to catch our breath, and once we stopped to pick up ourselves and the ladder after we both fell down.

It certainly wasn't any time to enjoy nature as a boy likes to do when he's out in a woodsy place. And of all things in the world, it wasn't any time for Poetry to start quoting a poem. But once, when the rain had let up a little, I heard him yelling as we puffed along with Poetry at the back end of the ladder and me at the front:

"I saw God wash the world last night
    With His sweet showers on high,
And then when morning came,
    I saw Him hang it out to dry."

It was a pretty poem, one I'd heard him quote at the Sugar Creek Literary Society, which meets once a month on winter nights in the Sugar Creek School.

So while we grunted and puffed and worried along, all the time getting nearer and nearer our rescue place, I let myself think about the rest of the poem, which Mom said is maybe the nicest nature poem she'd heard in a long time. The other four stanzas tell how, after the rain, blades of grass are all washed clean and so are all the trembling trees and the hills. The white roses are a cleaner white and the red roses more red since God washed their faces and put them to bed. Even the birds and bees were cleaner.

It was the last stanza I liked best, and which, because of the rain and wind, I couldn't hear Poetry quote very well, but it went something like this:

> "I saw God wash the world last night,
> And I would He had washed me
> As clean of all my dust and dirt
> As that old white birch tree."*

After I'd first heard the poem last winter at the Literary Society, every time I saw a birch tree I remembered the poem and felt kind of proud of the One who not only made all the growing things in nature but had worked out a plan for taking care of them—covering them over with a nice white blanket in winter and in summer washing them every now and then with rainwater, the best kind of water there is for washing anything, Mom says.

When we reached the overhanging rock where Little Jim and Dragonfly were, they dashed out to help us. But four boys carrying a light ladder is hard work, so we made them stop slowing us down and hurried on to the place where our end of the rope was still tied to the elm tree.

*William L. Stidger.

The first thing I strained my eyes through the filter of falling rain to see was Circus, down on the outcropping astride his juniper bronco. And my heart almost stood still. Our acrobatic, wonderful, almost-best boy in the whole territory wasn't there! The twisted trunk of the evergreen was still there, but Circus himself was gone!

What on earth had happened? And why? Had he lost his hold and fallen to the bottom and been killed on the rocks down there? I looked over the edge.

"Up here!" I heard Circus's cheerful voice call. "Not down there! I climbed up here to get in out of the rain!"

I looked and what to my wondering eyes should appear but Big Jim and Elsie *and* Circus, crowded into the hollow in the cliff that had been the lair of old Stubtail, the wildcat.

I also saw how Circus had managed to get there. The rope, one end still tied to the elm tree on our side, was hanging in a long loop down into the canyon. The other end was tied around the larger juniper growing on the ledge. I knew in a flash how Circus had managed it. Big Jim had secured his end, and Circus had caught hold of the rope and worked his way up hand over hand, the way mountain climbers do.

"Hurrah!" I heard Little Jim cry happily. "It's letting up! The rain's almost over! Look! The sky's starting to be blue!"

I looked toward the sky above the cliff wall and saw a wide blue field of sky as large as five acres of flax in bloom. In another few minutes, the afternoon sun would be shining again on the just-washed world.

It's a wonderful feeling, I tell you, to look at what a summer rain can do to the Sugar Creek territory. It makes it look clean and green and smell fresh and fragrant.

It washes a boy's heart a little, too—mine, anyway. And if he has his shoes on, he wants to take them off and go wading in the puddles, whooping it up and having the time of his life.

We tied our end of the rope to the top rung, and it took Big Jim and Circus only a few minutes to pull the ladder across to their side. We did have to be sure the spring locks were really locked before they began to pull.

That was when I noticed for the first time that Elsie was wearing a pair of brown shoes that looked as if they had rubber soles.

Poetry must have seen what I saw, because right then he said in my ear, "She was *carrying* the red shoes when she sneaked out of her up-stairs window. They'd have made too much noise, and she needed rubber soles for climbing."

"Yeah," I said back to him, "and she hadn't changed shoes yet when their car whammed into the bridge."

It looked as if our mystery was beginning to untangle itself.

Elsie had come to, and getting her across the extension ladder wasn't half as hard as we'd thought it might be. In fact, she didn't even need any help. It was as if she'd had a lot of experience climbing and doing athletic things.

I might have guessed that from the way she'd managed to get into and out of Old Man Paddler's upstairs window and also out of her *own* upstairs window at home, wherever that was.

I was surprised, though, that she didn't try to run away. That is, I was surprised until she said, "Let's hurry. Where does that doctor live, and how can we get to him the quickest?"

She looked pale, and her voice was trembling. Was it beginning to get husky? It did sound that way.

Big Jim made a quick decision. "One of us had better run on ahead and phone the doctor and have him meet us at Poetry's house. That's the closest place after we get through the cave."

"I will," Circus volunteered. He started to go, then winced, gritted his teeth, and reached down with both hands to his right knee.

Well, at a time like that, you can't wait around to decide who gets to do what. You have to decide who and what and get going. Circus couldn't make a fast run on ahead because he had wrenched his knee in his fall. Poetry was too big and slow. Little Jim and Dragonfly were out because of being the smallest. Big Jim had to stay and help Elsie, who had a twisted ankle beside being sick from the squirrel bite. So it got to be my job to race on ahead to the nearest phone, which would be at Poetry's house.

Even as I ran *lickety-sizzle* for the cabin and

the shortcut cave passageway that would take me to the sycamore tree and to Poetry's backyard, I remembered that once, a long time ago, I'd raced to *our* house and phoned Dr. Gordon in time to save Circus's father's life after he'd been bitten by a black widow spider. That's in the first story there ever was about the Sugar Creek Gang. It's called *The Swamp Robber.*

At Poetry's house I found a note on their back door, the one they use most.

Dear Leslie,

    We had to go to town for groceries. You know where the key is. Get yourself a snack if we happen to be late for supper.

                    M o t h-
er

I tried the door and found it locked. So, also, was every other outside door of the house. Now what? I could see the telephone on the wall not more than three feet from my face through their south window, but it was inside the house, and the window was closed and also locked!

Should I maybe break a window and climb in?

I decided to run home. Our house wouldn't have the door locked. And if it did, I'd rather break into it than into somebody else's house. I took out the pencil stub I always carry in my right pants pocket along with nails and stuff, and I scribbled a note below Poetry's mother's signature, telling the gang I'd gone home and why.

Then I took the shortcut through the woods, over the fence into our orchard, past the mound of dirt and the hole where the spruce tree would be set, around the corner of the house, and past the rain barrel that always stands there to catch the water that comes down the spout. I hardly noticed that it was full and running over from the rain that had just stopped a few minutes ago.

Mixy, our old black-and-white cat, was taking a catnap under the back step. When I came storming around the corner, she came to life and ran like a scared deer for the plum tree. She scooted up it as if I was a neighbor's dog.

I went into the house, letting the screen door slam behind me. There was no need to slow down and shut it like a gentleman. That's what I have to do when my folks are home.

I swooshed across the kitchen floor and into the living room and across its green rug to the telephone. First I stopped and listened, the way you're supposed to on a party-line phone, to see if anybody else was talking. If they are, it means the line is busy.

And the line *was* busy. So were two or three or four women. I couldn't tell how many, because they were all talking at the same time with maybe nobody listening to anybody.

Before I could interrupt to tell them I had to have the phone to call Dr. Gordon, I heard one voice that sounded like Dragonfly's mother's kind of excited tone saying, "Whatever are we coming to! So many teenagers are running away, over half of them *girls!* I just can't understand it!"

A lower-pitched, husky voice that sounded like Shorty Long's mother started to answer and got interrupted by Little Jim's mother. These three ladies alone sounded like seven or eight.

I broke in then, saying, "Excuse me, everybody, but I've got to have the line! I have to call a doctor. I—"

I mean I *tried* to break in. It was like trying to be heard above a zoo full of chattering monkeys. But I did hear something important, and I knew what had got them all stirred up to talk so much.

Somebody's girl over in Parke County had run away from home last night, and there had been a terrible auto accident at the covered bridge. Two teenagers had been killed, a third was in the hospital, and the other one had left her red shoes in the wrecked car and was gone nobody knew where.

Some of the things the women were saying stuck in my memory even though I wasn't trying to listen and maybe knew more about what they were talking about than they did.

"Just think," Dragonfly's mother squeaked. "I read in a magazine the other day that over three hundred thousand children run away from home every year, and twenty-four thousand of them go to California."

"Do you suppose they were running away to

get married? That's what everybody's saying."

"Not all of them," Little Jim's mother disagreed. "Not the Mayfield girl. She's too young. The radio just said . . . Oh, you didn't hear it? Well, it said her mother was a heavy drinker and was at the tavern when—"

That's when I really broke in. I started banging the phone and yelling loud enough to be heard as far away as the north road. "I've got to have the phone! We found Elsie up in the hills, and she's been bitten by a squirrel with hydrophobia, and I've got to call Dr. Gordon!"

Two of the voices answered me, saying, "Oh. Is that you, Bill?"

"Yes!" I yelled. "It's me, and I've got to call the doctor! Are you going to let me or not?"

7

I certainly hated to scream into the phone like that, but how else could I get their attention? Maybe that's the reason my little sister, Charlotte Ann, used to cut loose with such bloodcurdling screams now and then. It was the only way she could get her father or mother or busy big brother to realize she needed help. After all, she couldn't talk or anything yet.

Anyway, I got what I wanted, a chance to phone Dr. Gordon and tell him what I had to tell him and ask him to come quick. Because of all the other things that had almost stopped me that afternoon, I half expected the doctor's phone to be busy or that he wouldn't be at his office but out on a call somewhere.

But he answered right away in a strong, businesslike voice. "Thanks for calling, Bill," he said. "I'll be right there!" Even before he hung up, I heard him give an order to his nurse about something or other to pack in his bag.

Now I would make a beeline back to Poetry's house in time to tell the gang and Elsie, when they got there, that the doctor was on his way.

But I was only as far as our kitchen door when the phone rang our number. Deciding it might be important and hoping it wasn't one of the neighborhood mothers who had listened in and wanted to know more about where we'd found Elsie—and how was she, and had she really been bitten by a squirrel who had hydrophobia, and was she hurt in the accident, and how bad—I slid to a stop, rushed back, and said into the phone, "Hello. Bill Collins speaking!"

It was a good thing I had answered. It was my own deep-voiced father calling from halfway home from Memory City. There had been a bad storm, and a flash flood had washed out a bridge on the main road. I was to go ahead and do the chores and get myself a snack if he and Mom and Charlotte Ann didn't get home in time for supper.

Then Dad lowered his voice and asked, "You get the work done—you know—between the cherry trees?"

I hated to tell him the whole truth, so I decided to tell him only part of it, not wanting him to be disappointed. I would tell him the rest of the truth when he got home. Besides, it still might not be too late, after Elsie was taken care of, to hurry back to where we'd left the birthday gift in my red wagon only a few feet from Tennyson's chattering brook.

So I said, "Not quite yet. But it's a beauty! It'll look fine growing there!"

The telephone operator cut in then to tell Dad his three minutes were up, so he hung up.

Away I went again, through the kitchen to the back door and out, letting it slam shut any old way it wanted to. I ran past the ivy arbor at the side door, across the grassy yard and past the plum tree, past the rope swing under the walnut tree, and through the gate. Then I dashed past "Theodore Collins" on our mailbox and was off down the road.

Except that I wasn't running now. This time I was on my bike, pedaling furiously, knowing I could get to Poetry's house faster by riding on the road than if I took the shorter way on foot through the woods.

I wondered if we had acted fast enough to save Elsie Mayfield. My conscience told me I had acted as fast as I could, and so had the rest of the gang. But was it fast enough?

With the wind in my face and my shirt sleeves flapping, it felt a little like swinging in the high rope swing, but this wasn't any time to enjoy a fast bike ride. Pedal, pedal, pedal. Round and round and round my wheels flew.

I passed the north road, which, if I had turned right on it, would have taken me to the Sugar Creek bridge. I sped on to the hill and down it, across the little branch bridge, and up another hill toward Poetry's house. Sugar Creek was to my right, Poetry's woods to my left. On beyond were their barnyard and toolshed and, still farther on, the sycamore tree and the cave.

As I swung into Poetry's yard, I strained my eyes in the direction of the creek and saw through the trees a flash of red and knew it was the gang, bringing Elsie.

I leaned my bike against Poetry's white picket fence beside their gate and yelled, "Hurry up! The doctor'll be here any minute!"

That's when I noticed they were pulling my red wagon.

I thought, *Good old Gang! They're bringing Mom's birthday present too. It won't be too late after all!* Then I said out loud, "How in the world did they get it through the cave? They *couldn't* get it through!"

And that's when I saw there wasn't any cute little evergreen pyramid standing in a gunny-sacked ball of dirt in the wagon box. Instead, there was a red suitcase and a red blouse and a red pair of pants with a girl in them, riding along as if she was a queen and the gang was a five-horse team!

As soon as they were near enough for me to be heard, I called, "What did you do with Mom's birthday present?"

"Elsie has a sprained ankle," Big Jim reminded me, "so we let her ride. We took your tree out, put it in the shade, and poured a pail of water on the roots so it'd be safe to transplant tomorrow. We'll all go back and get it. We carried the wagon through the cave. We can do that on our way up tomorrow, too, to save time."

Forgetting for a second the most important thing—getting Elsie taken care of—I blurted out, "Yeah, but that'll be too late. Mom's birthday is *today!* I promised Dad I'd have it set out for her by the time he brought her home from Memory City."

What I'd just said seemed to bother Elsie. Maybe I made her feel sad because she had upset somebody's plan for a birthday surprise. She grimaced, shifted her position in the wagon, and said to me, "I'm sorry. I'm always spoiling everything for everybody!" I saw her swallow hard as if she had a lump in her throat and maybe an ache in her heart.

That is, that's what I thought it was at first. Then I remembered the rabies and got a scared feeling. That was another symptom of a patient getting hydrophobia. Along with a husky voice, it began to be hard to swallow. I was ashamed of myself for even mentioning the tree. Even though it was important, it wasn't half as important as saving Elsie.

This was the first time I'd had a good chance to look at her face, and do you know what? It didn't look at all like the face of a girl who was supposed to be such a bad girl.

Just when it seemed I'd better go in and call the doctor again to see if he had left, there was the sound of a car in the lane, and it was an ambulance with Dr. Gordon, another doctor, and a nurse. If it wasn't already too late, Elsie's life was going to be saved.

"Look!" Little Jim cried. "There's a rainbow! A double one!"

I think maybe I'd seen the rainbow myself but had had too much else on my mind to notice it especially. I cast a glance toward the northeastern sky and saw a wide arc spreading all the way across. It had all the colors of the spectrum with the red at the top of the arc, which is always the way it is in what is called a "primary" rainbow. The "secondary" rainbow wasn't half as bright as the smaller one but was maybe one of the brightest I'd ever seen with the red color on the *inside* edge, which also is the way it always is.

There was some fast action around us as the doctors took over. In only a few minutes they had Elsie in the ambulance and were about to drive away when there was a whirring sound in the sky. Swooping toward us out of the northwest from the direction of Turkey Run State Park was the helicopter.

Elsie, whose face I kept watching, looked startled and terribly worried. "It's my father!" she cried. "Don't start yet! Wait till he lands! There's something I have to tell him!"

There soon was not only fast action around Poetry's wide barnyard but there was sad action too. The short, red-haired father with a grim face and a tearful voice cried, and Elsie cried with him. He told her how sorry he was that he hadn't been a good father, and she begged him not to worry. She said that she'd be all right and that she loved him and that she shouldn't have run away.

At first her father wanted them to rush Elsie to the hospital in the helicopter. They could go swinging high over the hills and trees, cut across fields and roads, and get there twice as fast. The hospital was more than fifteen miles away at the county seat.

"She needs treatment right now," Dr. Gordon explained when he said no to Elsie's father. "We have everything she needs right here in the ambulance. We'll ride along and look after her on the way. I've phoned the hospital, and they'll have a bed ready."

It was pitiful—especially Elsie's worried face—when she asked the nurse, "Am I going to die?"

I didn't get to hear the answer, but whatever it was, it seemed Elsie believed it.

It was decided that her father could ride with the ambulance driver. The helicopter pilot, who had a flying service in Parke County and had been hired to help in the search, had finished his work and could fly back home.

Whew! What an afternoon!

It had been one of the most exciting afternoons of my whole life, and I was ready for a letdown. The only thing was, I couldn't let *up*. I still had the chores to do at home. And even though I had the best excuse in the world for not having the work done between the cherry trees, I hated to think of how disappointed Dad would be. We'd never be able to make it now—not even if we ran all the way to the cave, carried the wagon through, set Mom's birthday present in it, and pulled it as fast as we could back through the swamp.

I looked down at my empty wagon and heard myself actually sniffling as though I was little and had had a big disappointment and was about to cry.

Big Jim spoke then, and I noticed his voice sounded like a boy a lot older than he was. He said, "She was a nice girl. If she'd had a chance—if her mother loved the Lord Jesus, she would've loved Elsie too and wouldn't have spent her time in taverns. And if Elsie's father was a Christian, too, maybe he would've been home more, and they all would've been happy. If it were like that, maybe she wouldn't have wanted to run away from home."

I wasn't at all surprised to hear Poetry answer Big Jim, saying, "For want of a home, a daughter was lost!"

I guessed maybe Elsie had told the gang different things about herself when they'd been bringing her through the cave and all the way to Poetry's house. I also guessed that Big Jim and maybe the rest of the gang had talked a lot to Elsie, telling her about our having the Lord Jesus as our Savior and how He died for us and for her too.

Then Big Jim said right out plain and clear that my guesses were right. He grinned and told us that Elsie had believed in the Lord Jesus while they were still on the ledge and the rest of us were off getting the ladder.

Just then, the helicopter motor started. In a few minutes the giant whirlybird would take off. Then we'd be alone again with only each other, a red wagon, and, in the northeast, a rainbow that reminded us that God was still on

His throne and would be forever, just as He had promised Noah in the Bible right after the big Flood.

"All right, boys! Let's get going!" the helicopter pilot called.

"Get going where?" I called back to him and was astonished at his answer.

"We can get your tree and bring it back in time to set it where you want it for your mother's birthday present!"

How in the world did he know about the present?

I asked and found out that Elsie had told her father, and her father had told the pilot, and everything had already been planned. In a second, in spite of the worry in my heart for Elsie Mayfield, I felt as light as a feather.

There wouldn't be room enough in the whirlybird for all the gang *and* the tree, but there would be for Poetry, Little Jim, and me. That was the way it was decided as, half scared, we hurried to the helicopter to climb in and take our first whirlybird ride, high, high, and extrahigh above all the Sugar Creek territory up to Old Man Paddler's cabin and back again. If we really hurried, we'd have the cute little pyramidal blue spruce set and growing and I'd be out gathering the eggs when Dad and Mom came driving through the gate.

Boy oh boy, you ought to see Sugar Creek from away up in the air! The feeling I had as we swung out over the trees, the fields, and the creek itself, which was like a silver ribbon threading its way through the countryside below us, was a little like the way I'd felt a few years ago when I had gotten my first bicycle and was pedaling down the road on it.

The wind had been in my face that day too, and the flowers and weeds and trees flew past on either side. The only difference was that today I was almost half a mile high, and this time I didn't lose my balance and tumble out and bump my shins and my chin and get my knees all scratched up as I did on my bike.

In only a few minutes, we were landing in the open space between Old Man Paddler's cabin and his spring, just a short way from Tennyson's brook.

In another few minutes we had the soaking wet, gunnysack-balled, cute little blue spruce in the helicopter and again were up, up, up, and still up, making a wide sweep out over the swamp and heading for the Collins barnyard.

Little Jim said something as he sat beside me in the whirlybird that I knew I would never forget as long as I lived. He had both hands clasped around my right arm at the time, since there wasn't very much in a helicopter cab for a boy to hold onto.

The pilot had his eyes glued to his business, and Poetry, on the other side of Little Jim, was talking up to him about which controls did what, so I was the only one to hear what maybe was the nicest thing in the world for anybody to say.

Little Jim didn't say it to me, though, but to

the happy-looking little tree in front of him. This is what he said: "Listen, little tree. Don't you worry! And you don't need to be afraid even a little bit. You're just being transplanted. You're going to live in another place, and the Collins yard is as good a heaven as any tree could wish for!"

Then he settled back, leaned his small face against my arm, sighed, and said, "I sure am glad that Elsie is a Christian now, but I hope she doesn't get transplanted yet. You think maybe she will?"

I didn't have the least idea that Poetry had heard Little Jim's question, but he must have because he answered him. "Not yet, anyway. I heard Dr. Gordon tell the nurse they'd gotten to her just in time."

Then my heart did feel light. There wasn't a thing in the world to worry about, not one single thing.

Beside me, Little Jim came to life with a cheerful remark, saying, "There's the rainbow again! How come it's in the south now?"

But it wasn't. He had only gotten his directions mixed from whirling around in the whirly-bird.

For a few seconds I studied the fading rainbow, thinking how nice it would be if a boy could see a rainbow no matter what direction he was looking. Imagining what our minister might say if I told him what I had just thought, it seemed maybe he would answer, "You can, Bill, if you're looking up to God at the same time."

Our minister might say that. I'm pretty sure Mom would, if I happened to tell her.

I pulled my thoughts back inside the helicopter then to listen to something Poetry wanted to tell us. "How come nobody asks the detective about one of the most important clues in the red shoe mystery?" he asked.

"Everything's all solved," I answered him. "We know how she ran away, why she did it, where the red shoes came from, and—well, what else is there?"

"This," Poetry answered as he took from his shirt pocket the folded piece of newspaper from the classified section of the *Indianapolis News*. He spread it out on his lap so that Little Jim and I could read it.

I had forgotten about the paper, and I admitted it to Poetry. "But it's not important anymore," I said.

"But it is," he countered. "We know how she ran away and why she did it, but we didn't know where she was going. That is, we didn't know until I happened to see this. Read it!"

I leaned over, feeling my safety belt tighten from leaning across Little Jim. Poetry's finger was pointing to a want ad that had an almost invisible pencil mark underlining it, and this is what I read:

Unusual opportunity for teenage girls with plenty of personality. Travel, make money, get away from boredom.

As soon as Poetry was sure I had read the ad, he said, "My mother read a story about mothers and daughters one day last month. The story said every mother should warn her daughter *never* to answer an ad like that."

"Yeah," Little Jim said. He'd also been reading. "But what if the girl's mother doesn't care? What if she's like Elsie's mother?"

When he said that, I thought how my own cute little sister, Charlotte Ann, would grow pretty fast from now on. It seemed I ought to be glad she had Mom for her mother and that we had a whole family that belonged to God's family and loved Him and each other.

Below me now, I could see the walnut tree, the brown roof of our house, the green ivy that almost covered the window of my upstairs room, and the barnyard, where we were going to land in another few minutes.

And out on the west side of the house was a long pink row of hollyhocks, marching from the henhouse to a place halfway between the two cherry trees. By straining my eyes a little, I could see a mound of earth and, beside it, a hole in the ground just the right size to hold a birthday present for one of the best mothers in the whole world.

The *Sugar Creek Gang* Series: